Randy Kazandy

Where Are Your Glasses?

by Rhonda Fischer

Illustrated by Kim Sponaugle

This book is dedicated to
Randy Jacque,
the real Randy Kazandy
and the best storyteller I know.
And yes, he still wears glasses!
—Rhonda Fischer

Dedicated to my dad,
who always saw things so clearly.
—Kim Sponaugle

Special Thanks
To my family and friends, especially my sister
Judith for her creative inspiration and loyalty.
And to David who navigates marketing.

Hard Cover ISBN 13: 978-0-9820163-0-5 & ISBN 10: 0-9820163-0-1
Soft Cover ISBN 13: 978-0-9820163-1-2 & ISBN 10: 0-9820163-1-X
Library of Congress Control Number: 2008924636

10 9 8 7 6 5 4 3 2

Printed and bound at Worzalla Publishing, Stevens Point, WI in May 2010.

Published by Whim Publishing
31441 Santa Margarita Pkwy
SteA 308, Rancho Santa Margarita, CA 92688

www.whimpublishing.com
www.randykazandy.com
e-mail: info@whimpublishing.com

Cover & Interior Design by Jill Ronsley, Sun Editing & Book Design, suneditwrite.com

Child-safe! This book is printed with lead-free ink.

Randy Kazandy
loved to have fun.
He sang and he danced
in the light of the sun.

He ate like a champ
and grew like a weed.
His mom and his dad
were happy indeed.

As the months passed,
he grew stronger each day,
But his eyes couldn't focus
the usual way.

He walked in small circles.
He bumped into walls.

He couldn't read books,
and he always missed balls.

He stumbled and tumbled
for most of the day,
But this never stopped him
from wanting to play.

Mom said, "We must visit
the fun Doctor Bee
To find out why Randy
Kazandy can't see."

Randy and Mom
zoomed off in the car.
Doctor Bee's office
was not very far.

They entered the office, and what did they see?
A host of kids waiting for the good Doctor Bee.

The doctor declared, "Randy's eyes have some trouble.
The things that he sees are usually double.

"Randy Kazandy needs glasses today,
And then he can safely go out and play."

Miss Dibble set Randy's first glasses in place.
He suddenly made an odd-looking face.

He hated the glasses that sat on his face.
"I look like an alien who flew down from space."

Leaving the office, moody and glum,
He didn't want glasses—he thought they were dumb.

As soon as he could,
he'd get rid of them quick.
He wanted to lose them
before he was sick.

They wiggled and wobbled and slipped to the ground.
A car backing up made a loud crunching sound.

They were crushed! Now Randy had no specs to wear.
"Don't worry!" said Mom. "I bought four extra pairs."

When the next pair of glasses was placed on his face,
He knew that he had to get out of this place.

Down to the sandbox he scurried with glee
To hide the new glasses where no one would see.

He sprinkled the sand and some leaves as a cover—
But look who was coming. Oh no! It was Mother!

She picked up the glasses and shook off the sand.
"Randy! I'm tying these on with a band."

Back in the sandbox,
with glasses on tight,
Randy noticed a trash can.
The spot was just right!

Off came the glasses!
He tossed them up high
And wished those new glasses
would stay in the sky.

Into the garbage they fell with a crash.
The garbagemen swept them away in a flash.

Mother hurried outside, dropping her phone.
"Randy! I never can leave you alone."

Her hair stood up straight
as she looked in the bin.
This was a battle
she just might not win.

Randy gleefully called, "I have no specs to wear!"
"Come inside," Mom instructed. "I have a third pair."

When Mom drove the car to the grocery store,
The third pair of glasses smashed under the door.

She pulled the fourth pair of specs from a case,
And gently she placed them on Randy's small face.

Randy hopped in the cart and rolled past the fruit.
He grinned at a baby in a powder blue suit.

The little guy's mother was dressed in bright red.
"I'll sneak my new specs on that small baby's head."

When no one was looking, he took off his frames.
Randy Kazandy was still playing games.

As Mom passed the veggies and lady in red,
He slid his new specs on the cute baby's head.

Those glasses were not
the least bit in style.
"Let that little baby
wear them for a while!"

He rolled down the aisle
and waved his good-bye.
The baby now looked
like a big grown-up guy.

The fifth pair
of glasses
lay deep in
Mom's purse.
She reached in
to find them.
Oh, what could
be worse?

Mom put on the next pair of glasses with care.
"Don't be reckless," she said. "It's your very last pair."

At home she served Randy a slice of peach pie,
Saying, "Eat this, and please be a neat little guy."

Randy grabbed the last glasses
and pushed them down deep.
The fifth pair was now
much too messy to keep.

He couldn't wear his peachy new glasses like this.
Not even his mother would give him a kiss!

A knock at the door! Who had come? Doctor Bee!
Mom kindly invited him in for iced tea.

Doctor Bee held a box—Randy hoped it was candy,
But the doctor had known five more specs would be handy.

He said, "I won't stay because I'm in a hurry.
I brought your new glasses, so Randy, don't worry."

Doctor Bee left with a cheerful good-bye.
Randy lowered his head, and he started to cry.

Mom lifted him gently and put him in bed.
She reached for the glasses on Randy's small head.

Dad entered his bedroom and whispered goodnight,
Saying, "Randy, I, too, have had troublesome sight.

"How do you like my glasses? THEY'RE NEW!
Now I will look a bit more like you!"

"Can I choose different colors to make them more fun?"
"Of course you can, Randy. I'm proud of you, son."

He jumped up and down
and laughed with pure bliss.
"Without my new glasses,
the world I would miss.

"Now everything's clear! I won't bump into walls.
I can read all my books, and I'll have fewer falls."

"I'm **Randy Kazandy!** These glasses I'll keep!"
With a hug and two kisses he fell fast asleep.

Did you find all the glasses?

Please go back and look...

There is at least one pair
~ **somewhere** ~
on each page in this book.

"I love being me!"

~ In Loving Memory ~
Edmond Spencer Dibble Jr.
Spencer Joseph Dibble